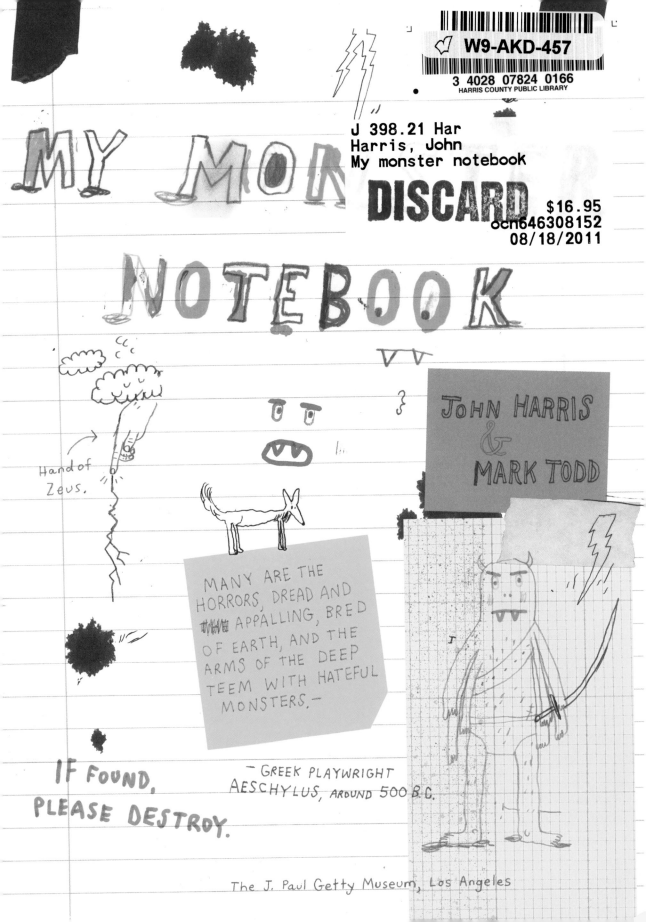

MY MONSTER NOTEBOOK

JOHN HARRIS & MARK TODD

Hand of Zeus.

MANY ARE THE HORRORS, DREAD AND ~~TWE~~ APPALLING, BRED OF EARTH, AND THE ARMS OF THE DEEP TEEM WITH HATEFUL MONSTERS. —

— GREEK PLAYWRIGHT AESCHYLUS, AROUND 500 B.C.

IF FOUND, PLEASE DESTROY.

The J. Paul Getty Museum, Los Angeles

Table of Contents

4

I ♥ MOM.

FAMILY.

X

DON'T EAT ME.

Echidna

CHIDNA WAS FAMOUS FOR LIVING IN a cave; she was also famous for being the mother of many horrible monsters and creepy creatures — Cerberus, the Sphinx, the Hydra — on and on.

Echidna was very beautiful from the waist up; below, she was a terrible serpent. She never got older; in fact, she was immortal — well, she thought she was: eventually she was killed by Argus-with-the-100-Eyes. (You'll meet HIM in a minute.)

Fun Fact There's an animal called an echidna — a real animal. Echidnas live in Australia and New Guinea. They're also called "spiny anteaters," which sounds dangerous....But they're actually gentle creatures. A baby echidna is called a *puggle*. Really.

(she's Beauty and the Beast.)

Welcome, my lovely
children.
Where is the
Crommyonian Sow?
I haven't seen
her in at least
100 years.

X CAVE DWELLER.

Orthrus and Geryon

R.I.P.

THE MOTHER OF ORTHRUS WAS (TURN back a page) Echidna. He was a dog with two heads. (His more famous brother, Cerberus, had three heads.)

Orthrus watched over the red cattle owned by his boss, Geryon, who had three heads, three bodies, but only two legs. Can you imagine?

Unfortunately for Geryon and Orthus, the great hero Herakles, famous for wearing a lion skin and carrying a very big club, wanted those red cattle for himself.

So much for Geryon and Orthrus.

THAT CERBERUS, ALWAYS ONE HEAD AHEAD.

Introduction to Mythology **15**

red cattle COW.

2 HEADS ARE BETTER THAN NONE.

ORTHRUS Good dog

DOG WITH 2 heads,

Briaereus

can you give me a hand?

HECATONCHIRES.

GESUNDHEIT.

100 HANDED.

LXIII =

CL

BRIAEREUS WAS—GET READY—ONE OF the three giant Hecatoncheires. This very hard-to-pronounce-and-remember name comes from the Greek, meaning "hundred handed." Guess how many arms they had, too? That's right. Plus fifty heads. Each.

Zeus liked the three Hecatoncheires: they came in very handy—ha-ha—in his colossal fight against the ancient race of Titans, who ruled the universe before Zeus took over. Just think of it!—they could throw three hundred huge boulders AT ONCE (100 arms each × 3 Hecatoncheires = 300 boulders).

Zeus later appointed Briaereus, his favorite, as his personal bodyguard. A VERY good choice, I'd say.

The three Hecatoncheires were associated with crashing waves and earthquakes. Can you guess why? I think you can.

18 *Introduction to Mythology*

ʒ THIS IS HANDS DOWN THE BEST DRAWING YET!

1 OF ʒ

50 HEADS × 3

50
× 3
+ 50 HEADS

WHEN YOU GIVE,
YOU RECEIVE.

BIGTIME.

Sorry.

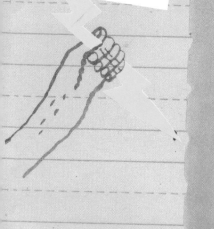

NOW
THAT'S
A
BIG
BIRD!

Ethon

ETHON WAS A HUGE, HUGE EAGLE: immense. Guess who his mother was. That's right.

Ethon is part of the story of the hero Prometheus. Prometheus gave the gift of fire to human beings, who up till then had been shivering in the dark. Prometheus didn't ask permission from Zeus to do this; Zeus, furious, chained Prometheus to a rock as a punishment.

It gets worse. Every day, Ethon, a huge eagle, would fly up to the rock where Prometheus was chained and tear out his liver—and eat it. Horrible! Then—during the night—the liver of Prometheus would grow back—and it would all happen again. Even more horrible!

This went on for a long, long time, until, finally, Herakles shot Ethon with an arrow and freed Prometheus, who must have been very, very, very grateful.

TOUGH
GUY.

Introduct

HERCULES!

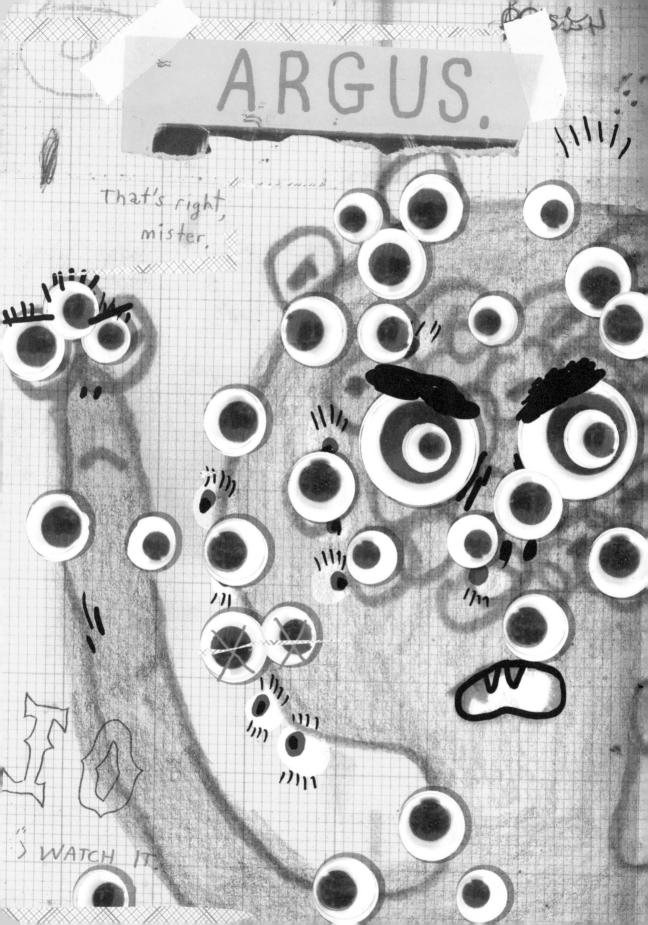

Argus

T HE FIRST THING YOU WANT TO KNOW about Argus is that he had 100 eyes. That's right: 100. Why did Argus need so many eyes? To keep watch over Io. Who was Io?

Io was one of the many, many female friends of Zeus, who—to keep her hidden away from his jealous wife, Hera—had turned Io into a cow. Yes, a cow.

But Zeus' trick didn't work. Hera, as usual, found out what was going on. She ordered her pal Argus to spy on Io-the-Cow. Argus could do this around-the-clock because two of his hundred eyes would sleep while the other 98 kept watch.

Zeus got tired of this situation and finally sent Hermes, messenger of the gods, on a mission to get rid of Argus. Which he did.

Hera took the 100 eyes of her dead friend Argus and placed them on the feathery tail of her favorite bird, the peacock. Which is why peacocks have what seem to be huge eyes all over their tails.

And now you know.

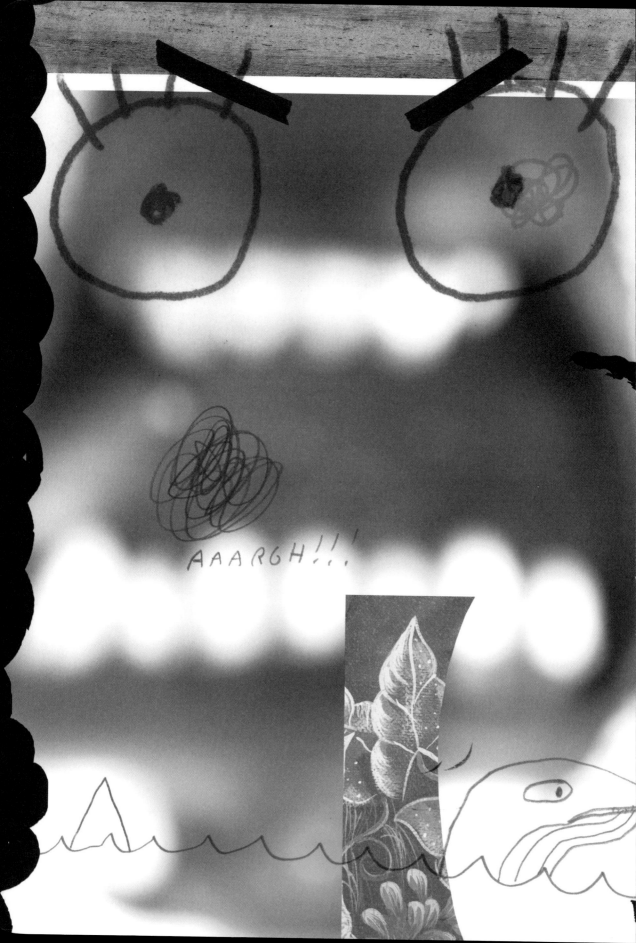

Keto

PAL OF LAMIA, MOTHER OF ECHIDNA HER OWN BAD SELF,

Lamia and Keto

LAMIA, LIKE ECHIDNA, WAS A VERY beautiful woman who happened to be a horrible serpent below her waist. She was famous for an awful reason: she would slink about at night, pouncing on kids who happened to be wandering around. Lock yours doors and be sure to keep Lamia at a big, big distance! You can't get much worse than Lamia.

Lamia was punished for her ways: some people say she couldn't ever close her eyes, so they were always wide open and she could SEE what she'd done—or was doing!

Lamia liked to hang around with Keto, another charmer: a sea monster who was the goddess of whales and huge sharks. Some people say that Keto was the mother of Echidna. What a family!

Fun Fact The great English poet John Keats wrote a long poem called "Lamia": "Love in a hut, with water and a crust!"

LOOK! IT'S THE LOVE HUT!

HUT 1, HUT 2,...

TOO CUTE?

CUNNING
SLY,

FOX.
∞
DOG.

The Teumessian Fox

BET YOU'VE NEVER HEARD OF HIM...
I know I never had till I wrote this book!
He was a fox—a **HUGE, HUGE** fox, and—guess
what?—yet another offspring of the dreadful
Echidna.

The Teumessian Fox ran around the city of
Thebes, terrorizing everyone. And no one could
figure out how to get rid of him, because his destiny
was never to be caught. By anyone. Ever.

The King of Thebes thought and thought
about this terrible problem. Finally he had a brain-
storm. He would turn lose the magical dog Laelaps,
whose destiny was to catch every single thing he
chased after.

Zeus, king of the gods, was now faced with a
tricky situation, fate-wise: if you have a fox who can
never be caught being chased by a dog who catches
everything he runs after, who is going to win?

Thinking about this gave Zeus a major head-
ache, and so he turned them both to stone. Which
is one way to solve a problem.

LAELAPS!

The Teumessian
Fox.

1961) (bibliography, 325 ff.); A. von Gerkan and W. Müller-Wiener, *Das Theater von Epidauros* (1961); *see also* ARCHITECTURE (all the books mentioned have sections on the theatre). T. F.; R. E. W.

THEBES (1) on the south edge of the east plain of Boeotia replaced, according to tradition, Orchomenus (q.v.) as leading city of Boeotia.

Recent excavat

find has revea
Mycenaean bui

Thebes was des

joined Athens and Argos

reece. For a brief period
as (q.v.), was the chief
egemony did not survive

3 Fox trot!

HUGE!

(A CLOSE CALL.)

NOW THAT'S A BIG FOX!

YEP.

LAELAPS

Hecate

 ECATE WAS KNOWN AS THE "GODDESS of the Crossroads" because she had three heads that each looked in a different direction. One was a dog, one was a snake, one was a horse. As if that's not spooky enough, she was often shown with ghost dogs beside her as she walked about at night, sometimes holding a torch in each hand. Yikes!

She was called the goddess of witchcraft and spells and the "Queen of Ghosts"—which is pretty scary; on the other hand, she was the goddess who looked after women who were about to have a baby—which was a very good thing.

Fun Fact Shakespeare mentions Hecate in two of his best plays: *A Midsummer Night's Dream* and *Macbeth*.

1. DOG
2. SNAKE
3. HORSE

34 *Introduction to Mythology*

TOUCH GHOSTS.

SHAKESPEARE.

ghost dogs,

MR. FROSINI DREW THIS.

HELLO, GOODBYE.

Typhon

TYPHON WAS TERRIFYING, EVEN BY monster standards. He had a hundred monster heads, which we've seen before, only **HIS** hundred heads touched the **SKY**, and nasty venom dripped from his hundreds of eyes, and red-hot lava poured out of his hundred mouths, which also hissed and roared. Could it get any nastier?

He and Zeus, king of the gods, were terrible enemies, and when they fought, they nearly destroyed the entire earth, as they picked up whole mountains and threw them at each other.

Just as Typhon picked up Mount Aetna (a real mountain, in Sicily), and threw it at Zeus, Zeus zapped him with a hundred thunderbolts, and Typhon **DROPPED** Mount Aetna, which landed on top of him, pinning him underneath. Which is where he still is, and which is why Mount Aetna still spits out rocks and lava and smoke to this day. Some call it a volcano, but we know it's really Typhon, who's still mad.

Fun Fact He had many monster children by—guess who?—that's right. Who else would it be? Echidna.

Ssss....

Mt. Aetna

Science Book of

VOLCANOES

↳ Not good.

TW-1359

gush.
ROAR... ROAR!!!
TYPHON
drip-drool.
gurgle.
HISSSS....
HISSS....
grrr...
gurgle-gurgle

Thought you could get away with it, didn't you?

GOTCHA.

Erinyes

HE THREE TERRIBLE ERINYES WORE crowns made out of snakes—and that's just for starters! When you add the eyes dripping blood, the bat wings....Yikes!

Why were the Erinyes so scary—I mean, aside from the dripping blood, etc.? Because they stood for **VENGEANCE**—capital V. If someone did something wrong, especially something really wrong, the Erinyes would soon be swooping in for a visit, and then—look out!

The Erinyes were also known as the **FURIES**. By whatever name you called them, they were punishers.

Look out below!

AHHHHH!

Proteus

PROTEUS WAS A SON OF THE SEA-GOD Poseidon and his nickname was "The Old Man of the Sea." He liked to hang out in Egypt and splash around with the seals, who were some of his favorite animals.

Proteus had a special talent: he could see the past, the present, and the future. But he didn't like to talk about them!

Many people came to Proteus with questions about **THEIR** past, **THEIR** present, and **THEIR** future. When he wouldn't talk, they'd grab hold of him and try to force him to tell his secrets. And it was at this point he would turn into—anything. Anything you can imagine. From a monster to a lion to a tree to a roaring fire.

If you managed to hold on through all this, and not lose your grip, he'd return to his usual shape and answer your question.

But not until then.

BEFORE.

AFTER.

SPLISH - SPLASH!

SPEAR ME THE DETAILS!

grrr...

Cacus

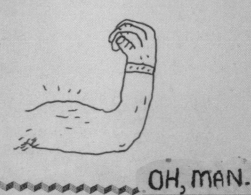

CACUS WAS A FIRE-BREATHING MONSTER who lived in a cave where the city of Rome now stands. He scared everyone; he'd scare you, too: if anyone came too near his cave, he'd drag them inside and the next thing you knew, he'd be nailing that person's head to the door.

Like so many monsters, Cacus met his own end at the hands of Herakles. Cacus tried to hide inside his cave; Herakles—not one to mess around—ripped off the top of the cave and jumped inside.

Before too long, Cacus' head was probably nailed to the door, too.

OH, MAN.

Circle

CIRCE WAS NOT A MONSTER, TECHNICALLY speaking; most people say she was a beautiful lady, a queen who ruled over her own island.

What is Circe doing here, then? She's here because she was famous for turning men into monsters and beasts by her use of magical plants and herbs.

The great hero Odysseus met Circe on his wanderings. Her huge house was surrounded by lions and wolves (hmmmm....), and at dinner she turned most of Odysseus' fellow travelers into pigs. Odysseus himself managed to escape this fate and eventually find his way back home, but not everyone was so lucky, as all those lions and wolves and pigs could tell you, if they could talk.

Fun Fact Circe has been very popular with writers and painters and other artists. Now that you know who she is, you'll probably notice paintings of her in museums and see her name in books and poems. Artists tend to like her because she was so **INTERESTING**.

I think that I
SHALL NEVER SEE
A POEM LOVELY
AS CIRCE.

LIONS
WOLVES
PIGS.

CIRCE.

A.

CONCH
SHELL.

½

Triton (and tritons)

RITON (LIKE PROTEUS) WAS A SON OF Poseidon, God of the Sea, so it's not surprising he was half-man, half-fish. You may have seen pictures or statues of Triton: he's usually shown carrying a trident (a three-pointed spear) and a big twisty conch shell, which he'd blow on like a trumpet. It was so loud it startled everyone, even the gods on Mount Olympus.

Triton lived in a palace at the bottom of the ocean, which is spooky to think about. He gave his name to the "tritons," who were, needless to say, half-man (or half-woman), half-fish. Not as big as Triton himself, the tritons were more like aquatic pals who would splash around in the water beside some bigger god or goddess.

Graeae

T HERE WERE THREE OF THESE ANCIENT women—three sisters who really were gray. Their Greek names are impossible to remember (for me, anyway), but their names, in English, were: Dread, Horror, and Alarm. Wouldn't you like to run into them on a dark night!

It gets even creepier. The story goes that the three Graeae only had one eye and one tooth between them and so they had to PASS AROUND their one eye and one tooth—take turns!

One day the great hero Perseus stole their single eye when they weren't, so to speak, looking….He needed some information from them, and he got it!

21

number 41

#8

50.

11

STAR STUDENT,

No 19

40

5

31

Nereids

HERE WERE FIFTY OF THEM, ALL daughters of Nereus (which is where they got their name). Though unusual, they weren't really monsters, but they provide a pleasant break after the Graeae.

The Nereids were lovely sea nymphs who lived with their father in a cave at the bottom of the sea, and they were famous for helping sailors when their ships were caught in storms. You could do worse than be a Nereid.

They had some very unusual names, even for mythological beings. Here are a few:

AUTONE	OPIS
BEROE	PHYLLODOCE
CALLIANASSA	PLEXAURE
CRANTO	PLOTO
EVARNE	SPIO
HIPPONNOE	THOOSSA
IAERA	

35

3

3

38

DOUBLE JOINTED.

number 4

3

48

26

Introduction to M

GOOD SINGER.

5

13

39

PLAYS A GOOD LYRE.

NO,

16

BEST JUGGLER,

GAME
OVER

Talos

TALOS LIVED ON THE ISLAND OF CRETE and he was **BIG**; very, very big. And made out of bronze. Instead of blood in his veins he had molten lead, which is very strange to think about. His blood flowed from his bronze neck right down to his bronze feet. To keep the blood-made-of-lead from flowing out, Talos had a big plug in his big ankle. Can you guess what's going to happen?

The hero Jason and his companions came sailing by Crete one day in their ship, the Argo (which is why Jason's companions are called the Argonauts). Jason and the Argonauts needed to stop and get some fresh water, but Talos wouldn't let them. So Jason came up with a sneaky plan. There are different versions of the plan in the ancient stories, but they all end the same way: Talos is tricked and before he knows it, the plug in his ankle has been pulled out and all his molten blood is flowing onto the sand.

End of Talos.

Introduction to Mythology **53**

We're thirsty.

A

DELPHI

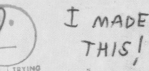

I MADE THIS!

→

Dear

Python

PYTHON—AS YOU MIGHT EXPECT—WAS a snake: a very dangerous female snake who lived in Delphi, an extremely famous spot in ancient Greece. Her sworn enemy was the great god Apollo. Why?

Hera, the wife of Zeus, sent her pal Python to get rid of baby Apollo. The plan didn't work, but baby Apollo grew up and didn't forget what had happened. Eventually he tracked down the Python to her cave at Delphi, and that was the last of Python.

Fun Fact Python's name comes from the Greek word meaning "to rot."

Dear PYTHON,
You stink.
x Apollo
xxoo

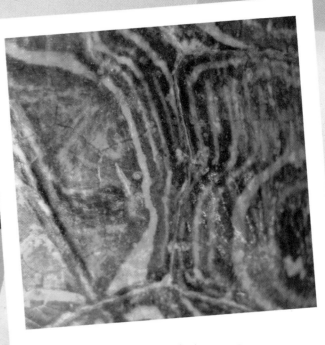

Goodbye.

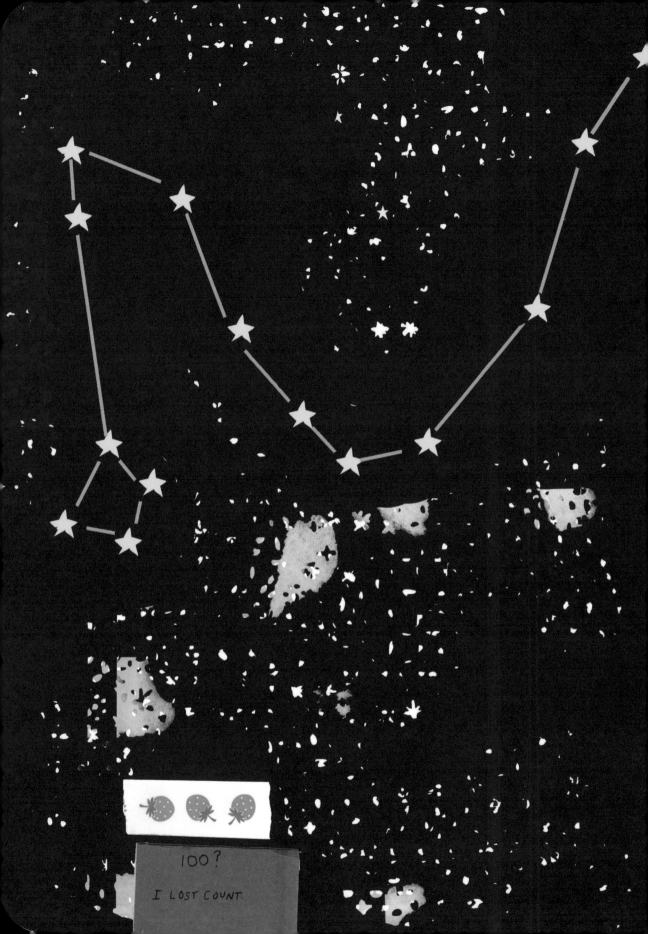

MAJOR
CLAWS!

2

Ladon

LADON WAS A HUNDRED-HEADED dragon with a hundred voices, too, who ended up among the stars in the sky. How?

Ladon guarded the tree with beautiful golden apples in the Garden of the Hesperides, which was far, far away, at the end of the world.

Major hero Herakles was given the task of finding those golden apples and bringing them back, and to do that, he had to dispose of Ladon and his hundred heads. Which he did.

Once Ladon was dead, he was put in the sky as the constellation Draco. Which means dragon. Which makes sense.

REMEMBER
THE GOLDEN RULE.

AN
APPLE A
DAY
KEEPS THE
LADON
AWAY.

HOW YOU SAY IT.

Pronunciation Guide

Names are arranged alphabetically for ease of reference.

Aeschylus.............. **ES-kuh-lus**
Aetna.................... **ET-na**
Briaereus.............. **bree-eye-RAY-us**
Cacus .... **KAH-kus**
Cerberus.............. **SIR-ber-us**
Circe.................... **SIR-see**
Delphi .... **DELL-fee**
Draco .... **DRAY-co**
Echidna .... **eh-KID-na**
Erinyes .... **eh-REEN-ees**
Ethon .... **EE-thon**
Geryon .... **GARE-e-on**
Graeae .... **GRY-eye**
Hecate .... **HEK-a-tee**
Hecatoncheires...... **hek-a-ton-KYE-rees**
Hera .... **HARE-a**
Herakles .... **HARE-a-klees** really?
Hermes................ **HER-mees**

THANK
YOU.

MESSED
UP,

Hesperides	**Hes-PAIR-ih-dees**
Io	**EYE-o**
Keto	**KEE-toe**
Ladon	**LAY-don**
Laelaps	**LAY-laps**
Lamia	**LAY-mee-a**
Nereid	**NEER-ee-id**
Odysseus	**oh-DISS-ee-us**
Orthrus	**ORTH-rus**
Poseidon	**po-SYE-don**
Prometheus	**Pro-ME-thee-us**
Proteus	**PRO-tee-us**
Talos	**TAH-los**
Teumessian	**Too-MESS-ee-an**
Thebes	**THEEBS**
Typhon	**TIE-fon**
Triton	**TRY-ton**
Zeus	**ZOOSEs**

Real name: unknown
Age: unknown
height: 3ft. 1in.
weight: 3½ pds.
weapons: none
Enemys: Butch
Friends: none
owner (?) found

rating: 6
Strength: 1

Shagg

INASTIVE

© 2011 The J. Paul Getty Trust

Published by the J. Paul Getty Museum, Los Angeles
Getty Publications
1200 Getty Center Drive, Suite 500
Los Angeles, California 90049-1682
www.gettypublications.org

Project Staff
John Harris, Editor
Jim Drobka, Designer
Elizabeth Chapin Kahn, Production Coordinator

Printed and bound by Tien Wah Press, in Singapore (W626302)
First printing by the J. Paul Getty Museum (12400)

Library of Congress Cataloging-in-Publication Data

Harris, John, 1950 July 7-
   My monster notebook / John Harris ; illustrations by Mark Todd.
      p. cm.
   ISBN 978-1-60606-050-6 (hardcover)
1. Monsters--Juvenile literature. I. Todd, Mark, 1970- II. Title.
   GR825.H32 2011
   398.21--dc22

                    2010025302

GOOD   WORK

Enter Ne~~ptune~~ Poseidon

Have no conniptions, Bacchus, And as for you Leander,

Nestor approaches... No tarrying, my boy!

Lightning lights the sky with awesome lightning

Zeus is angry..... Everybody duck!